BRIAN'S

JOURNEY

- A Novel

Merril E. Holloway, II

BRIAN'S JOURNEY
Copyright © 2018 by Merril E. Holloway II
© by Sheila Hayford, Cover Design, Editor, Formatting, Publication
©http://www.whatawordpublishing.com

Published by Dr. Sheila Hayford, What A Word Publishing and Media Group.

All rights reserved. No part of this book may be reproduced or transmitted in any form or by any means without written permission from the Publisher.
Publisher requests should be sent via email to Dr. Sheila Hayford at: info@whatawordpubublishing.com
or via contact form at www.whatawordpublishing.com.

This is a novel and therefore some of the characters, towns and events are fictitious. Real life events in the book will not have the real names.

ISBN 978-1-7328240-9-6

Printed in the United States of America.

Dedications

I dedicate this book to:

- My parents, Bazola Holloway and Merril Holloway Sr. My mother always had a positive attitude and gave me encouraging words when I wanted to quit. My dad taught me to have a strong work ethic. Mom and Dad, thanks to both of you for believing in me.
- My nieces and nephew: Kendall, Kenny, Kimberly, and Kayla. You guys mean so much to me. This book is a testament to your impact on my life. I hope you live your life to the fullest.
- All my readers who have been told that you cannot attain your goals and desires in life. Continue your quest to find your purpose.
- God, the Almighty, who makes all things possible.

Merril E. Holloway, II

ACKNOWLEDGEMENTS

I would like to acknowledge and thank my uncles, Mr. Leather Thompson Jr. and Mr. Duwayane Thompson, for always encouraging me to be great.

I would also like to thank my sister, Mrs. Charlisa Edelin. It is truly a blessing to have such a caring and loving sister. You always keep me grounded and provide me with that needed push. Last but not least, I would like to thank my better half, Morgan Brodeur. When I need that push you are right there to give me one.

Merril E. Holloway, II

ENDORSEMENTS

"Merril possesses a genuine goodness of heart. You can be assured that what Merril is saying or doing is coming from a place of truth within him. He has consistently shown the courage to confront and overcome the obstacles in his path. Goodness, Truth, Courage; these are rare commodities. In Merril you will find all three."

Mr. Kenneth Edelin.

Merril is an inspirational Author and Motivational Speaker who enlightens the mind and soul. And so I say with the Apostle Paul in the book of 2nd Corinthians Chapter 9 verse 10: "Now may the God who supplies seed to the sower and bread for food, supply and multiply the seed you have sown and increase the fruits of your righteousness."

Tracy. A Miles.

Table of Contents

Dedications 3

Acknowledgements 4

Endorsements 5

Foreword 7

When Life Throws You a Curve Ball 8

So You Think Education Is a Joke 19

Barely Getting By 29

What Are You Scared Of? 36

Facing Reality 42

It's A Marathon 55

What Do You Want out of Life?................. 67

Facing Your Greatest Fears 81

Taking Advantage of Opportunities 95

Making Excellence Happen 100

Meet The Author 119

Meet The Publisher.................................... 121

Foreword by Charlisa Edelin

Brian's Journey is the story of a young man's journey through life. Like many of us, Brian had real fears of failure and rejection. Unfortunately, some of those fears came true. However, Brian teaches us to persevere through those tough situations to reach a goal.

Everyone can relate to Brian's story. Who has not had to face a challenge head on in order to reach a goal? Brian's struggle - reading - is a common problem among low achieving students. Since so much of our curriculum is based upon reading, a poor reading acumen will almost certainly turn into poor performance in school.

However, Brian turned around his fate. He tackled his fear of reading and writing and graduated from a college student who was kicked out of school for poor academic performance to a college instructor with a Master's Degree. Brian's story will inspire you to never give up and realize that none of us is too old to learn and change.

When Life Throws You a Curve Ball

Brian's Early Years

Brian's father remembered the day as if it were yesterday: After a slip and fall into Lake Michigan during a fishing trip before Brian was born, he had a vision of a son. Gaining renewed strength from this powerful image, his father was able to swim ashore. Brian's father felt that his son was a major reason he was still alive.

Chapter One: When Life Throws You a Curve Ball

The summer season was coming to an end as the fall leaves began to change colors. The lack of humidity made it the perfect day for Mr. and Mrs. Anderson to take their daily evening stroll around their subdivision in Waukegan, Illinois. Pregnant with her second child, Mrs. Anderson's baby boy was due any day now.

Suddenly, Mrs. Anderson felt a pull, then a contraction. "Honey," she said, "I think the baby is coming now!" The second-time parents-to-be hurried back to the house, packed Mrs. Anderson's overnight bag, and drove straight to the hospital. Late that evening Mr. and Mrs. Anderson's son was born. *They named him Brian.*

Brian was a bundle of joy that his whole family adored. Emily, his older sister, was especially excited about this new addition to the family. She had always wanted a playmate and was already thinking about all of the enjoyable games she and her brother would soon play together.

Several months after Brian's birth, his family packed up and moved to the state of Washington. Since Brian's father was in the military, his family would move whenever an opportunity for advancement became available or duty called. Each move gave Brian's father a promotion; this move made Mr. Anderson a Private First Class in the Army. Although Brian was too young to remember this move, later on in life he did recall memories of moving around a lot during his childhood years.

As always, Mrs. Anderson was excited to experience life in another state. Brian's mother was grateful that her children were fortunate enough to experience the traditions of other cultures through opportunities that most people would never experience during their lifetimes.

Six year-old Emily was also eager to move to another state. "In our new house, mommy, I will help you to take care of my new brother!" six year-old Emily told her mother enthusiastically.

After two years in Washington, Brian's father informed the family that they would be relocating yet again, this time to the country of Turkey. Brian was a young child and did not understand that he would be living in a country far away from the United States. However, it did not seem to bother him. Brian only wanted to be with his family and enjoy the ride.

Located near the Mediterranean Sea, Brian's family moved to Ankara, Turkey. The citizens of Turkey seemed to look up to America because it represented freedom, and many longed for their country to embrace that same freedom.

From the start, the people of Turkey were welcoming and treated the Anderson family with respect. Brian's dad, for some reason, became a celebrity with the locals. On one occasion, Brian's father was invited to a Turkish wedding. This was unusual at that time because the Turkish people did not usually invite people from other cultures to family events.

At the age of four, Brian was not yet able to attend school, so his family hired a Turkish woman named Mina to help take care of him. Brian was an active boy who longed to play all day and watch cartoons. However, the family did not have a television while living in Turkey. Brian did not like that he was no longer able to watch his morning cartoons. Instead of watching television, his parents, as well as Mina, read books to Brian and his sister. They also listened to music to pass the time. Brian's family also participated in activities and events that involved other military families in order to acclimate themselves with the culture of this new location. To keep Brian occupied, his mother also enrolled him in year-round sports clubs.

One day while Brian and Emily were playing outside, a large dog charged toward them. When Brian noticed that the dog was foaming at the mouth, Brian had no idea what to do. As Brian ran into inside to call for help, Emily made sure that the dog did not follow her brother into the apartment building. Before their help arrived, the dog bit Emily's left arm. When they found out that the dog had rabies, Emily had to get many preventive immunizations. Brian's dad was very upset and told his son that he should not have run when he encountered the dog. His dad explained that running from a dog could have made the dog chase after him.

This situation taught Brian that he must always be prepared for the consequences of his actions. Through his sister's courageous deed, the young man also learned that it is often better to face, rather than run from, your fears; in the end, running away may cause more harm than good.

* * *

As a military family, life was predictively unpredictable. One day, Brian's father came home and announced to his family that they would be moving once again. After living in Turkey for two years, the family packed up and moved back to the United States, this time to North Carolina.

In North Carolina, Brian made many neighborhood friends. Each day after school, Brian and his new friends would play outside until dinnertime. Most of all, Brian loved playing football and riding his bike down the giant hills in the subdivision with his neighborhood gang.

Brian's father taught his son to ride a bike during their first summer in North Carolina. During riding lessons, his dad would hold onto the bike's handlebars as Brian focused on balancing and pedaling at the same time. On one occasion, Brian crashed right into two trees and popped the front tire of his bicycle. Despite a few "bumps in the road," Brian became an expert bike-rider in no time at all.

During the summer months, Brian always looked forward to visiting his grandparents; Mr. Anderson's mother lived in Louisiana and Mrs. Anderson's parents lived in Alabama.

Brian's favorite cousin, George, would always come along on their road trips to Alabama to visit with their grandparents. Brian and George were best buddies and had been inseparable as far back as they could remember.

Each day upon returning from school, Emily and Brian would watch cartoons while eating their afternoon snack. After snack, they would finish their homework before Mrs. Anderson arrived home from work. By the time Brian was in second grade, Emily noticed that it was difficult for Brian to finish his homework before his mom got home. She noticed that he was struggling the most when it came to reading second-grade texts. These observations led Emily to believe that her brother was having trouble learning to read. Therefore, Emily took it upon herself to help Brian with his homework every afternoon.

One day, Emily told her mother about Brian's intense difficulty with completing his reading homework. Brian's second grade teacher, however, never noticed the warning signs of Brian's learning disability. If she did, this concern was never communicated to his parents. Due to their busy work schedules and lack of knowledge about learning disabilities, Brian's parents also did not see the warning signs that Emily saw with his reading. It was not until later in his schooling that this need would be addressed.

After returning to the United States and being back for two years, Mrs. Anderson was beginning to wonder if her family was done with relocating for a while. If so, she was ready to make some long-term plans, like building their own home in North Carolina.

Several days later, Brian's father informed his family that they would be moving to Germany the following month. With that in mind, while still hoping that it was too good to be true, Mrs. Anderson's was forced to put her plans for building her southern dream house on hold.

By this time, Brian had made many loyal friends and was sad that he had to move again. As a young child, moving to another country and leaving behind familiar friends and faces was difficult for Brian. He was frustrated by the frequent pattern of leaving his old friends and being forced to make new ones. The Anderson family left North Carolina the summer before Brian's third grade year.

When a military family relocates, they are often placed in temporary housing until they are assigned to their "permanent" residence. Attaining permanent housing was often a slow process that involved being on a waiting list. The duration of time spent on the waiting list fluctuated and was based on availability. While on this waiting list, the Anderson family's temporary residency was located on the fourth floor of an apartment building. Although it was difficult to carry groceries, books and bags up four flights of stairs, the Anderson family adjusted to this new routine.

When he was not climbing the steps to and from his apartment building, Brian spent a considerable amount of time with his new neighborhood friends. His friends in North Carolina were soon distant memories.

Brian's third grade year began with a test to assess his literacy skills. Brian despised reading and was upset that his teacher was making him take such a hard test so early in the school year. Brian's teacher reviewed the results of her students reading assessment and assigned students to reading groups on the second day of the school year. All students, except for Brian, were assigned to a peer group. After reading the members of each group aloud, his teacher approached Brian, who was confused that his name had not been called for any of the student groupings. "You will have to read with me. You are not in trouble, I would just like to give you a little extra help with your reading," she told the discouraged young boy. This comment left Brian feeling sad and dumb.

When the class went outside for recess, Brian's classmates began teasing him about having to read with the teacher. Brian went home that day and cried. When Emily asked her brother why he was crying, Brian complained to his sister about being the only student assigned to read with his teacher and that he was embarrassed. He also told her about how he had been teased during recess. Emily consoled her brother and told him to ignore the teasing. She also expressed that he would have to work a bit harder if he truly wanted to improve his reading fluency. During dinner that night, Brian told his parents about his day. After reiterating Emily's message, his mother added, "Go to school and do your best. Everything will be alright in the end."

This experience helped Brian to realize that his real friends would never make fun of him. His real friends accepted Brian for who he was, learning disability and all.

* * *

The family's permanent residence was an apartment located within walking distance of Brian's school. Emily's school was directly across the street from Brian's. Brian and Emily would walk to and from school each day with their neighborhood friends.

Brian frequently thought about his sister's acknowledgement of his reading difficulties. "This isn't a new problem," Brian would say to himself. "Why is Emily the only one to notice? Maybe I would be smart if someone decided to help me." Brian was sure that his struggle with reading in school didn't just start in the third grade.

In the month of February, Brian's third grade teacher requested a parent-teacher conference to discuss Brian's academic progress thus far in the school year. She explained that Brian seemed to have a trouble with developing his foundational literacy skills. His teacher described the supports that would be provided to Brian in order to improve his reading skills. She assured the young boy's parents that she was determined to help Brian to be successful. Mr. and Mrs. Anderson now realized that everything that Emily had expressed about Brian's reading difficulties were true. They were dumbfounded that his previous teachers had not mentioned or provided intervention strategies to help their son achieve academic success.

After the conference, Brian's mother and father believed that with hard work he could catch up with the other students. Their goal was to help their son to gain confidence in his reading skills. Although his parents continued to provide him with encouraging words, Brian felt that his best would never be good enough.

Thankfully, with the help of his third-grade teacher, Brian was able to read grade-level texts by the end of the school year. He was ecstatic that his hard work had paid off. His parents, as well as Emily, were extremely proud of Brian. They understood that school was a struggle for him and that this accomplishment proved that Brian had strength and determination needed to overcome his academic challenges.

Sometimes life throws you a curve ball. When it does, draw on your strength and learn to stay the course, just as Brian did.

So you think Education Is a Joke

Brian's adolescent Years

When Brian's father asked his son what he wanted out of life, Brian would tell his dad that he wished he could go back in time and change his feelings and negative thoughts about his education.

Chapter Two: So You Think Education is a Joke

When he was twelve years old, Brian's father came home one evening with a surprise announcement. With great excitement, Brian's father told the family that they would be moving to Newburg, Germany, which was a five-hour drive from their current residence.

Emily was less than thrilled about this news. Brian's sister was about to begin her senior year of high school and was upset that she would have to make new friends and meet new teachers. In addition, she was devastated that her reign as Senior Class President was ending before it even started. However, the most troubling part for Emily was the fact that her new school would be the big rival of her current and familiar school. That summer, the reality that she would be playing sports against her friends began to sink in as the family moved to their next destination.

Brian prepared for his seventh grade year at his new school. As he transitioned into his middle school years, Brian was nervous that academics would continue to be a struggle.

* * *

After moving to Newburg, Brian encountered a group of boys around his age playing football. Brian was ecstatic when his new acquaintances invited him to join their game. When Brian arrived home that evening, he told his parents all about his day. "I know I am going to love it here! My friends don't even notice that I am not good at school!" Brian instantly knew that he was going to enjoy his time in Newburg.

One day while Brian and his friends were playing football, a kid asked if he could play with them. Brian's group ignored the young boy's request as they continued their game. Brian knew how it felt to be the new kid in town, so he left the game to ask the boy if he still wanted to play with them. The new kid from Texas, whose name was Jason, eagerly accepted Brian's offer. Brian and Jason began to hang out with each other every day. *This was the beginning of a life-long friendship.*

* * *

Brian quickly found a group of guys from his school that he enjoyed hanging out with. Brian and his friends thought it was cool that the older boys at school had named their groups, or "crews". The young boys decided to start their own "crew." They decided on the name "The Junior Boyz" based on the fact that Brian and his friends were all named after their fathers. In normal crew fashion, "The Junior Boyz" had personalized jackets made. Brian and his crew enjoyed the added attention that they were receiving from the young ladies at school.

* * *

During her final year of high school, Emily was striving for straight A's as always. She had her eyes set on her goal of earning a college degree. Brian, on the other hand, was just getting by in his studies. However, he did not feel that he was struggling academically despite the all too familiar "C's" that his report card presented.

Neither of Brian's parents had graduated from college. As a result, they wanted their children to receive an education so that they could make a better life for themselves than they did. Mrs. Anderson would constantly say to Brian, "Education is important." However, Emily's constant recognition and Brian's lack of praise from his parents made him believe that he wasn't the college-type.

* * *

At the age of thirteen, Brian asked his parents if he could get a job. Brian was tired of asking his parents for money; he was tired of the never-ending inquiries about what he "needed" to buy. After his dad got him a job at a nearby supermarket, Brian worked bagging groceries (for tips) every Saturday. Brian enjoyed having a steady income that he could spend on whatever he wanted. As the only one in his crew with a job, Brian hated that he was missing out on his friends' many Saturday adventures.

Brian's father noticed his son's frustrations. He sat Brian down and explained to him the importance of working hard. "Although you may not see it now," Mr. Anderson lectured, "your hard work will pay off in the long run. It will be more rewarding than you even realize."

* * *

Studying for tests was a challenge for Brian. Brian did not care to learn the proper test-taking techniques. Despite his mother's unwavering encouragement, Brian also despised reading. Unfortunately, his embarrassment about his reading difficulties prevented Brian from asking for much-needed help. Surprisingly, Brian was able to pull off a passing grade in the majority of his classes.

Brian frequently procrastinated on his homework until the day it was due. In the morning before first period, Brian and his friends would find the "smart kids" and convince them to let "The Junior Boyz" copy their homework.

Brian's father wanted his son to be a great student because he personally had not taken advantage of his educational opportunities after high school. He wanted his son to get a good education because he knew it would be important to him later on in life.

Brian's mother was always on him about getting his schoolwork done. Brian hated when his mother would nag him about school. He knew that he was struggling academically and did not want or need someone to constantly rub it in his face.

* * *

After getting to know each other, Brian and a young lady named Shannon quickly became an item. Along with the title came an end to Brian's already minimal concentration on his schoolwork. This became a huge problem with his parents. Not surprisingly, Brian's sister did not have the same conversation about school with their parents because she was an outstanding student.

Brian began to resent Emily because their mother would always brag about how smart his sister was. It was hard for Brian to understand that he should not compare himself to his sister. He was not able to believe that he was just as smart as his sister. To Brian, being a good student was not an attainable goal.

* * *

When it came to the world of culture, Germany was about six months behind the United States. Taking advantage of this, Brian and his friends would always bring back to Germany the latest American fads (usually music) after their hometown visits.

On a summer trip to visit family in Louisiana, Brian and his father discovered a candy that was just released in the United States. They were an instant hit in the States. This gave Brian a grand idea: "What if I brought these back to Germany and sold them to all the kids?" Mr. Anderson thought the business proposition was a good idea so Brian and his father went to the neighborhood store and bought every box of the candy they had.

The candy came in small packages that cost ten cents per pack. Mr. Anderson and Brian sat down and came up with a plan. They decided to charge twenty-five cents per pack so that they could make a profit.

When Brian arrived back to Germany, he told his friends that he had brought back a new candy and was selling them at his house. Brian was becoming "the man" and all the kids thought that this young entrepreneur was the coolest.

Brian's new business gave him the confidence that he was unable to attain from his below-average academic achievements.

* * *

Brian's summer was coming to an end. When they received their schedules, Brian and his friends discussed their upcoming eighth-grade classes.

Brian's English teacher was Mrs. Webster. Brian and his crew had heard that Mrs. Webster was very strict and held her students to unachievably high standards. Brian did not want to believe this rumor because he was determined to have a successful school year. To make things worse, Brian could no longer get help from his sister because Emily was away studying Journalism at Happy Valley University.

Since he did not have to work as hard in his other classes, Brian tried his best to focus his energy on his English class. Brian's English grade at the end of the first nine weeks was a solid "D". This devastated Brian to the point where he wanted to give up on school altogether. When she saw his report card, Mrs. Anderson had a long talk with her son about the importance of education. Brian tuned his mother out, as always, because he did not want to hear what she had to say.

When it was time for parent-teacher conferences, Mrs. Anderson's only objective was to find out what it would take for her son to succeed in his academics. Mrs. Webster explained that Brian would have to work and try harder in class if he wanted to improve his grades.

Mrs. Anderson came home from the conference and explained to Brian what his teacher expected from him going forward. Brian did not want to talk about school with his mother because he felt that she was always comparing him to his sister, Emily. Brian knew he did not have good study habits. He wanted to do well in school but would frequently "shut down" when presented with a challenging academic task. Brian did not believe that the hard would pay off, especially in his difficult English class.

During their discourse concerning Brian's education, Mrs. Anderson knew that Brian had checked out of the conversation. She then said to him,

**"You may not hear what I say today,
but one day life is going to show you what it is all about.
Right now you think education is a joke,
but you won't be laughing if you don't get yourself together."**

Barely Getting By

Brian's High School Years
Part I

Mrs. Anderson would always say to him: "One day, being the class clown will come back to haunt you." However, up to this point, Brian was enjoying the attention he received from his high school peers.

Chapter Three: Barely Getting By

Brian's last year of middle school was uneventful. The real excitement began with the start of his high school years.

Freshman Year

In Brian's mind, popularity was more important than his academic success. As a result, the majority of his time and efforts were spent on becoming a member of the "Cool Kids Club." However, membership to this elite group came with certain requirements. Brian had to prove that he could hang out with the "cool kids" by passing a series of tests.

The first test, making fun of people based on whatever flaws they had, was a breeze for Brian. He was a natural at making people laugh at the expense of others. Brian himself was insecure about his academic abilities and height (he was 5 feet, 5 inches on a good day) so making fun of others made him feel superior.

As Brian and his friends walked through the main lobby of the school, Brian commented on anything and everything that would cause embarrassment for the individuals he encountered. Nobody was safe when it came to Brian's jokes. Physical appearance and fashion taste were his specialties; Brian's remarks about overweight girls wearing skinny jeans made his peers laugh until their stomachs ached and helped Brian to pass the first test.

The next test took place in the classroom setting. The goal was to do something funny in class while the teacher was teaching. Brian thought long and hard about how he would accomplish the task because he did not want to get in trouble with his parents. He knew that this would be a hard test to pass; standing out in the hallway making jokes was one thing but interrupting a figure of authority went against the values that his father had instilled in him.

* * *

Brian's hesitation in executing this task stemmed from a past experience. After throwing a chair at his first grade teacher, Brian's father reprimanded him in front of all of his peers. The embarrassment that he felt over a decade earlier remained in the back of his mind. Since then, Brian had worked hard to rebuild his father's trust and he was afraid to lose it over his selfish need to be well-liked.

* * *

One week went by and Brian could not find an "appropriate" opportunity to accomplish his second test. Each morning the founding members of the "Cool Kids Club" would ask Brian about his current status.

"Did you do what we told you to do? Because nobody in your class has come to us and reported it," a member asked of him one day. Brian sheepishly responded, *"Nope, haven't had the time. Don't worry. The whole school will be talking about it real soon."*

Brian did not know if he was waiting for the perfect time to strike or if he was scared of the punishment he would receive from his parents. Either way, the members of the elite group were beginning to question Brian's loyalty to the cause.

One day Brian finally found the perfect moment. On a dreary rainy day, Brian's classmates all got a whiff of a distinct odor that no one could trace to a specific area of the room. No one, that is, except Brian. He was certain that the mystery smell radiated from his classmate, Angela, who sat adjacent to the anxious jokester.

The moment was right! The class was silently completing their assignments as Brian blurted out, *"Oh, my gosh! What is that smell? Someone smells like fish!"*

The whole class immediately burst into laughter. Brian's no-nonsense teacher demanded that Brian step out of class as punishment for his disruptive behavior. Brian walked out of the classroom feeling proud. Brian knew that Angela was his good friend and that the situation was very embarrassing for her. However, at that moment Brian was not concerned with her feelings because he longed to be part of the "crew." Angela was so devastated and embarrassed that she decided to miss school for the next few days.

Once word got back to the other guys, Brian forgot about the possible consequences he could face with his parents. Although it came at an uncomfortable price, Brian was confident that he would be initiated into the clique.

There was now one final test for Brian to pass to become a member of the "Cool Kids Club." The leaders told Brian that he had to find a way to embarrass a classmate in the cafeteria. Brian thought about it and felt he had a plan for the best prank in the history of the clique. For a week Brian went to lunch to map out his plan.

Brian waited for the best time when all eyes and attention would be on him. Tim, a kid that was picked on by everyone, was carrying his tray of food. As Tim was about to sit down to enjoy his lunch, Brian tripped him. The whole cafeteria began to laugh at Tim as his food flew across the room. The cool kids gave the prankster a "thumbs-up" at the same moment Brian realized the Principal had been in attendance of the show that had just occurred.

Mr. Johnson called Brian to his office. Without giving the Principal a chance to talk, Brian blurted out that the previous events were an accident. Of course, Mr. Johnson did not buy his lie. Brian's joy in his accomplishment was quickly replaced with the fear of his mother and father's reaction to his well-deserved one-day suspension.

Mr. and Mrs. Anderson were not amused by their son's conduct. They explained to Brian that they sent him to school to learn, not to act like a fool. As punishment, Brian had to clean the entire house. He also had to write a heartfelt letter of apology to Tim. Mr. and Mrs. Anderson contacted Mr. Johnson and asked if their son could read his letter to Tim aloud in the cafeteria. Like his parents, the Principal thought that this was a fair consequence for Brian's thoughtless actions.

* * *

Sophomore Year

Brian was still struggling in high school because he did not want to study for his classes. English was Brian's favorite because Mr. Washington would show movies in class and rarely gave homework. Brian and his peers had to turn in a journal entry every Friday. Week after week the routine was the same; the students would display their assignments on their desks as Mr. Washington walked around the classroom. A passing grade was given as long as a finished product was shown. Brian knew that Mr. Washington was not paying close attention to the assignments so he began to reuse his journals from previous weeks.

Brian's minimal efforts were pretty consistent across all academic areas. For now, playing basketball was the focus of Brian's time and energy.

Later in life, Brian would come to realize that barely getting by in school would play a significant role in his journey.

WHAT ARE YOU SCARED OF?

Brian's High school Years Part II

The week of basketball tryouts arrived. All of the sophomore guys were hoping that they would make the team. Everyone that is, except Brian.

Chapter Four: What Are You Scared Of?

Basketball tryouts were all Brian's friends could talk about when the flyers went up around their school. Brian, however, was nervous about trying out for the team.

Brian did enjoy playing basketball with his neighborhood crew but was unsure of his skills compared to those of his peers. When asked, he confirmed that he was indeed trying out for the team. However, he knew that he was not going to try out because he was afraid of defeat.

Brian thought long and hard of excuses he could use to avoid the upcoming tryouts. He went to his job and asked if he could work extra hours during that particular week. This way he could use work as his excuse for not trying out for the basketball team.

On the day of the basketball tryouts, Brian's friends (once again) asked if he would be in attendance. Brian told them that "unfortunately" he had to work and could not get out of it. Of course, this was only an excuse to avoid rejection and disappointment if he did not make the basketball team.

* * *

Junior Year

The summer before their junior year of high school, Jason and Brian spent endless hours working to improve their basketball skills at the neighborhood courts. One summer night after a long day of playing ball, Jason made a comment about how they would be the star players on the basketball team during the upcoming school year. Brian sat silently. As his confidant, Jason could sense Brian's doubt in his athletic abilities.

"Brian, you know you're just as good as the other guys. *What are you scared of?"* Brian responded, *"Man, I don't know why I get so fearful when it comes to believing in myself. Maybe I'll try out for the team this year."*

* * *

Basketball season was soon approaching. Brian remembered his tryouts experience, or lack thereof, of the previous year. All of the guys were once again talking about going out for the basketball team and they asked Brian if he was going to try out for the team this year.

The week before basketball tryouts, Brian was overwhelmed with the same feelings of uncertainty that he had felt the previous year. To avoid the possibility of defeat and rejection, Brian searched long and hard for a legitimate excuse not to try out for the team once again. After having a lot of difficulty in creating an excuse, Brian rode the bus home on the day of tryouts.

At the bus stop the following morning, Jason asked Brian why he was not at the tryouts. Brian sheepishly replied that it was his mother's fault; she ordered him to come home right after school because his grades were not good enough for him to play on the team. His friends knew that this was a complete fabrication but left the topic alone.

Once again Brian was missing out on one of his passions because he could not muster up the courage to try out.

* * *

Senior Year

Jason had played high school basketball for the past two years and was a basketball sensation. Although he enjoyed cheering for his best friend, it was painful for Brian to attend the basketball games.

Each game was a reminder of Brian's unwillingness to step out of his comfort zone and to face his fears.

However, this year was different for Brian. Once football season was over, the same flyers for basketball tryouts were posted all around school. The same conversation began again and this time the guys did not say anything to Brian because they assumed he would not be trying out. When Brian walked into the gym for tryouts, Jason and the rest of the guys were surprised to see him.

Brian gave it his all during tryouts. He knew that this was his last chance to prove to his buddies, and himself, that he had the skills to play on the school basketball team. For the first time he felt confident in his talents. He hoped and prayed that the coaches were impressed with his confidence and what Brian brought to the court. Tryouts were over and the waiting game had begun. Those that tried out for the basketball team were anxiously waiting to find out if they had made the team.

* * *

The moment arrived and the results were posted on the outside wall of the gymnasium. Brian slowly walked up to the list to find the location of his name on the basketball team roster; however, *his name was nowhere to be found.*

Brian was speechless. As his friends celebrated their spots on the team, Brian felt like he was hit and knocked down by a tornado.

"After all these years, I finally got up the nerves to try out and what did it get me? Cut from the team. I knew I shouldn't have gone to the stupid tryouts."

After all was said and done Mr. Kennedy, the head coach, explained to Brian that his performance during tryouts was impressive; the coaches agreed that he was one of the best point guards they had seen during tryouts. However, the coaches wanted some of the freshmen boys to sit on the bench to see what was expected of the players. The bus ride home was a long and difficult ride. Brian went home that night and cried himself to sleep. Brian returned to school the following day. Feeling overwhelmed and defeated, he asked the basketball coach if he could be part of the team in some way. Coach Kennedy appointed Brian as the team's statistician.

Brian finally faced his fear of rejection.
He was devastated that the results were not what he expected. However,
Brian was still proud to be part of the team.

FACING REALITY

BRIAN'S COLLEGIATE YEARS PART I

Despite Brian's carefree attitude toward school, he did enough to survive and complete his K-12 education. After high school graduation, Brian moved to the United States to begin his college career at the University of Principles. It began to sink in that Brian was one step closer to discovering what the "real world" would be like.

Chapter Five: Facing Reality

After graduating from high school, Brian moved back to the United States to live with his sister in Virginia. In addition to her full-time journalism job, Emily worked part time at an athletic store called "Racquet and Jog." Due to Emily's reputation as a hard worker, the assistant manager at the athletic store was more than willing to offer her college-bound brother a job for the summer. In addition to his job at "Racquet and Jog," Brian spent the summer working toward his goal of attaining a driver's license.

In Germany, a young person could not receive a driver's license until the age of seventeen. Brian graduated from high school when he was seventeen so he decided to wait to get his license until he was back in the United States. The state of Virginia requires soon-to-be drivers to pass both a written test and a driving test in order to attain a driver's license. Brian took the written test and he passed with flying colors. Although he was proud of his accomplishment, he knew the real test would be the upcoming driving portion. Brian had minimal practice driving on actual roads in Germany, so he experienced intense anxiety when faced with this unfamiliar and difficult task.

The day came for Brian's driving test. While waiting for his name to be called, Brian filled his thoughts with positive affirmations.

"You can do it," he told himself over and over again.

When the officer called his first and last name, Brian's heart dropped down to his stomach. He quickly rose from his seat to meet the officer. The moment he had been waiting for had finally arrived.

Brian and the officer got into the car that Emily graciously let her brother borrow. As Brian approached the edge of the parking lot, he had difficulty seeing the street in his field of vision. As a result, Brian drove his car slightly past a stop sign. The driving officer immediately demanded that Brian stop the car; he explained that Brian had failed the driving test. Brian felt tears trickle from his eyes in disbelief. Brian was devastated. In his young mind, this setback confirmed that he was a failure at everything in his life.

Unfortunately, Brian had become accustomed to this reality.

* * *

During the summer, Mr. Anderson retired from the Army and relocated to Alabama to be closer to Mrs. Anderson's parents. As summer was coming to a close, Brian traveled from Virginia to Alabama so that his parents could drive him to his freshman year of college. Since Brian did not get his driving license in Virginia, he thought he would attempt to achieve his goal one last time in Alabama.

Since he had taken his first driving test in another state, Brian had to take the written *and* driving tests *again*. He went to take the written portion and, like the first time, passed on his first attempt. Brian now found himself in the same predicament he faced before: passing the written test and unsure if he would pass the driving portion of the test. This time, Brian would make sure that he stopped at every stop sign he approached. This time around, Brian was faced with a huge obstacle; he would have to drive his grandmother's car which was long in length compared to his parents' car and it had shifting gears.

During the driving test, everything was going smoothly until Brian had to make his first turn. Due to the length and overall size of the car, Brian attempted to make the turn cautiously. Despite his best efforts, Brian hit the curb with his grandmother's car. The officer immediately turned to Brian and said the words he dreaded to hear: *You've failed!*

Brian had to wait a week before he could take the driving test again. A week went by and Brian went to take the test again; this time he passed with flying colors. And so, finally, Brian got his much anticipated driver's license.

When faced with the reality that life would not always go his way, Brian persisted and refused to give up on his personal goals.

* * *

After Brian's great accomplishment it was time for his parents to drive him together with his belongings to the University of Principles. Located in Texas, Brian chose this college because this was the school his best friend Jason had chosen. Brian and his dad packed the car the night before so that they could get an early start on the road. The trip from Alabama to Texas would be a long one.

As Brian and his parents set out on their journey, Brian reflected on his mediocre efforts in high school. Despite beginning his college career on academic probation and the expectation that he would maintain a 2.0 grade point average each semester, he was determined to work harder over the next four years of his education.

* * *

Freshmen were required to move in a week before the start of their classes in order to participate in freshman registration and orientation activities. Upon arrival to the University of Principles, Brian's family met up with Jason and his mother to check into their shared dorm room. As they were setting up their personal items, Jason and Brian were introduced to their other roommate, Tim. While helping her son organize his belongings, Brian's mother kept glancing in Tim's mother's direction. Several minutes later, the two women realized that they had grown up in the same Illinois town. The two families laughed and reminisced about life in the old days.

During the week of orientation, freshman students were required to take a college placement test to determine which remedial classes students needed to take or skip over. The focus of remedial courses was to improve students' basic skills before moving on to their major-specific courses. Brian despised standardized tests.

He felt they were overly difficult and left a bad taste in his mouth. Brian spent the night before the test hanging out and playing video games with Jason and his new dorm mates.

Rather than facing his fears and learning from his mistakes, Brian continued to undermine the importance of his education.

On testing day, the Proctor handed out the assessments and stated that each student had two hours to complete the test. Upon receiving his test, Brian immediately fell asleep on his desk. About an hour later Brian awoke and began his assessment. When he was finally in the groove, the proctor announced that the two hour testing window was over. "Stop writing, put your pencil down, and close your testing booklet. I will now come around and pick up your test." Brian barely completed half of his test so the possibility of doing well was slim. As expected, Brian's scores were below average so he was required to take all remedial courses during his first semester at the University of Principles.

* * *

After spending a few long days moving their son into his dorm, Mr. and Mrs. Anderson began their trip back home to Alabama. Brian and Jason said goodbye to their parents before taking a walk around campus. It was during this nightly stroll that Brian and Jason realized that they were finally on their own. Brian turned to Jason: "Man, we can make our own decisions now." "Yea, that's right!" Jason said in response. Although it was getting late, Jason and Brian went upstairs to change their clothes so that they could go play a late night game of hoops.

Brian's college schedule was extremely different from the 8am to 3pm high school courses he had grown accustomed to. He now had three classes on Mondays, Wednesdays, and Fridays and only one class on Tuesdays and Thursdays. This was a strange concept for Brian because he was not used to having "free time" during the school week. He was not sure how to handle his newfound freedom, especially because his parents were hours away and were not lecturing him on how to use his time productively.

Brian was living the "life," or so he thought. No one was telling him what to do, when to study or when go to bed. This, to Brian, was the best life ever! Any extra time Brian had during the day would be spent playing video games in his dorm room, playing basketball, or catching up on sleep after late night hangouts with his dorm mates.

* * *

Brian learned his first important life lesson within his first week of living the college life. After an afternoon of basketball with some freshman guys, Brian hungrily walked to the dining hall. Eager for his evening meal, Brian arrived at the dining hall around seven o'clock. It was then that Brian realized that the dining hall had already been closed for an hour. Brian's first lesson was simple: If you miss dinner, don't expect to eat until tomorrow.

* * *

Brian and Jason took notice of their roommate's diligent study habits early on in the semester. Tim, who was in the engineering program, would routinely take time out of his day to read and/or study for his classes. Jason and Brian would joke about how the "smart kids" in college would add study time, rather than social time, into their daily schedule.

Brian and Jason, on the other hand, focused their time and energy on anything and everything that did not involve academics. Although Brian attended all of his classes, he did not dedicate any time outside of the classroom to his studies. Brian's mother would call periodically to check up on her son and his studies. Brian's response was always the same: "Everything is going well and classes are good." Brian would always feel bad after these phone calls with his mother because he knew he was not telling the whole truth. He also knew that his mother was able to see through his lies. Although she knew that her son was not telling the truth, Mrs. Anderson never questioned Brian's motives. She allowed her son to experience the freedom that came with life in college; *she knew that sooner or later Brian would have to face the reality of his decisions.*

* * *

Brian's first semester of college was drawing to a close. Although he was excited to spend time with his family in Alabama, Brian was anxious about receiving his grades for this semester. He wanted to make sure he had the opportunity to review his grades before his parents got a hold of them.

Brian knew that first semester grades would sent home in the mail during the week of Christmas. Every morning, Brian would wait impatiently for the mail to be delivered to his house. Upon its arrival, he would walk to the mailbox and check the mail before his parents came home from work each day. By the middle of the week Brian's anxiety was higher than ever. Finally, while sifting through the mail on the Thursday before Christmas, Brian came across an envelope that was inscribed with the emblem and address of the University of Principles. Brian paused in his garage and ripped open the envelope. After a quick glance at his grades, he realized that he had maintained the necessary 2.0 in all of his classes. Brian could not contain his relief and excitement. He jumped up with joy and shouted an emphatic, "Yes!" Brian then called his friend Jason; he was even more thrilled to find out that Jason, too, had received passing grades in his college courses.

As soon as his parents arrived home from work that evening, Brian barely said hello before showing them his passing grades. Brian's parents took him out to dinner that night to celebrate his accomplishment and the completion of his first semester of college.

* * *

The five-week winter break came and went. Upon returning for their second semester at the University of Principles, Brian and Jason signed up for their classes.

Brian enjoyed his Physical Education and Spanish courses. Science, however, was a huge struggle for Brian throughout his second semester of his college career.

Since it was a prerequisite course for both of their majors, Jason and Brian decided to sign up for the same Biology class. As was to be expected, this was not a good idea. The two jokesters spent more time clowning around than they did on their classwork, homework, and test preparations combined.

Although they did not spend much time with their roommate, Brian and Jason continued to take notice of Tim's intense study habits. The two best friends would make jokes about Tim not having a social life or being as "popular" as them. Just like in high school, Brian enjoyed making jokes because it took the attention away from him and his mediocre academic success. Brian would later realize that asking Tim to teach him his study habits would be more beneficial than making fun of him.

Despite his lack of interest in his education, Brian's second semester was another "good" one; he barely maintained his 2.0 grade point average. Satisfied with his efforts, Brian boarded the plane that would take him home to Alabama for the entire summer.

Brian would soon realize that no matter the obstacles he had already encountered, he would continue to face the challenges that life presented to him.

Mrs. Anderson would always say to Brian, "The race is not given to the fastest nor the strongest but it is given to the one who endures."

It's a Marathon

Brian's Collegiate Years
Part II

Brian's parents were optimistic about their son's future. He maintained a C average throughout his first two years of college, so it seemed like he had a good handle on his studies. Yet, Brian's good luck would soon come to an end.

Chapter Six: It's a Marathon

At the end of the summer, Brian headed back to campus to begin his sophomore year at the University of Principles. Mr. and Mrs. Anderson drove Brian to school and helped him set up his dorm room, just as they had done the previous year. Delighted by the brilliant and successful young man their son was becoming, Brian's parents said their goodbyes and then reminded him just how blessed and proud they were to be his parents.

* * *

Bright and early the following day, Brian walked to the University of Principles Registrar's office. Upon entering the building, he spotted the *Register for Classes Today!* sign and eagerly positioned himself at the back of the line. When it was his turn to register, Brian kindly stated his name and handed over his list of classes to the woman behind the registration desk. As the woman began to input Brian's information into the computerized registration system, she paused.

When she finally spoke again, she looked up at Brian and explained his unfortunate predicament. "Brian Anderson, I'm afraid you have a hold on your registration.

You'll need to go and see your Dean in the Business department. Have a nice day."

Have a nice day? Brian thought. ***How will I explain this to my parents?***

Brian maintained a puzzling look on his face as he walked all the way to the building that housed the University of Principles School of Business. Brian was aware, through rumors and his own brief interactions with her, that the Dean of the Business department was a woman with a very stern disposition. Dean Rose's top priority was to create one of the best post-secondary Business schools in the region.

As he sat in the lobby and anticipated the horrible news he knew he would be receiving, a tall and confident figure approached Brian. "How can I help you?" Dean Rose asked of the young man seated in front of her. "Uh, well, the lady at the registration desk told me to come and see you because there is a hold on my registration for classes," Brian sheepishly replied.

Dean Rose, without another word, led Brian to her office. As she directed Brian to take a seat, she sat behind her computer and immediately began typing away. It seemed like it took a long time for her to see what the issue was. She said, "Unfortunately, I have some very bad news for you. As you already know, you were accepted to the University of Principles on *academic probation*. This means, as was explained to you upon acceptance to our university, that students on probation *must* maintain a grade point average of 2.0 each semester. I am looking at your grades from the spring, and it seems that you only achieved a 1.8 GPA."

"What does that mean then?" Brian asked with a muffled voice. Brian already knew what the answer to his question would be. However, he was hoping that maybe, just maybe, Dean Rose would offer a solution that did *not* involve an awkward phone call home. "You cannot attend our university this semester." Dean Rose replied with a strong, yet sympathetic, tone. "No Dean Rose, please! I can't go back home to my parents. Isn't there something else you can do? I mean, I am *only* two-tenths of a point away from a 2.0!"

"Unfortunately, sir, there is nothing I can do, I am very sorry. I hope to see you back in the spring."

* * *

Brian's walk back to the dorm felt like an eternity. Although he wanted to act like everything was normal, deep down he knew that he had no other option but to face his friends and let them know what was going on. Brian walked into his dorm room and, after realizing that he was alone, fell on his bed and let the tears roll down his cheeks. As he freed his body of the emotions he had kept bottled-up since receiving his fate, he heard the turning of a key followed by the presence of a familiar figure.

It was Jason. "Yo, did you get your classes?" Brian took a deep breath and relived the day's events with his best friend. "No, I can't register this semester because I didn't meet the requirements." The news shocked Jason. However, the look of disbelief on his face was *nothing* compared to the feeling of embarrassment that Brian was experiencing.

* * *

After facing his confidant's reaction to the news, it was time for the hard part; the inevitable "I screwed up" phone call home. In addition to explaining how he had let his mom down, he also needed to ask for a ride home to Alabama.

This, by far, was the worst day of his life.

The tears resumed as he dialed the number for his parents' landline. Brian wondered how his parents were going to react to the whole situation. After the fourth ring, Brian's question was about to be answered. "Hello?"… "Mom, it's me."… "Hey baby, is everything ok?"

"No, mom, it's not. I went to register for school and they told me that I had to come home for a semester."

By this time, Brian's trickling tears had become a full-fledged cry. "Oh no, Son. What happened?" Brian recounted the whole story as his mom listened intently and silently. When he was finished, Brian's mom responded in a soothing tone. "It will be okay. Just come home and we will talk about it later."

Brian's parents sent him a ticket home for the following day. Since Jason had a car on campus, he offered to drive his friend to the airport. The car ride was silent and filled with gloom as the two best buddies drove to the airport and said their goodbyes.

* * *

Back in Alabama, Brian spent most of his time fantasizing about all of the fun he and Jason should be having: playing basketball, card games, and, most importantly, checking out all of the hot girls on their dorm floor. Brian's father, on the other hand, was ready for his son to start living in the present. "While you are here, you are *not* about to sit home all day, every day. Go out and get a job!"

Brian knew that his dad was right. While the idea of wasting the day in front of the television appealed to him, Brian could feel himself falling deeper into a state of depression. He realized that he must pick up the pieces and put his life back together again if he wanted to return to the University of Principles in the spring.

Brian found a job at a nearby clothing store and worked about thirty hours per week. Although Brian realized that he needed to make his school work a priority if he was to return and graduate from the University of Principles, Brian did not take full advantage of his time off. He spent much time reflecting on the benefits of hard work and discipline; however, he did not focus his time on learning the skills needed to be disciplined in his work and to create good study habits.

* * *

The day Brian was waiting for finally arrived: the start of the spring semester. Brian's parents, once again, bought him a one-way ticket to the University of Principles. After spending the past few months at home, Brian was ready to show his parents that the money they were putting toward his education would not be wasted. He knew that he needed to start to take his studies seriously. After all, Brian was still on academic probation and *did not* want to be sent home from school ever again.

Brian and Jason decided to branch out from their comfort zones and began to hang out with a new group of people. The majority of their "new" friends were on academic scholarships, which Brian found very ironic given his academic struggles. Brian was hopeful that hanging out with this group of high-achievers would have a positive effect on his studies. He did not want his new peers to think that he wasn't smart so he did his best to work as hard, if not harder, than they did.

Brian and Jason's new friends were avid readers. Wanting to fit in, Brian hid behind the façade of an intellectual. Brian tried to read the books that they were reading so that he could join in on their scholarly conversations. However, due to his personal struggles with reading, he realized that reading took too long for him.

Although he enjoyed spending time with his new and intellectual friends, Brian longed to reunite with his basketball and video-playing posse. As an unfortunate result of his shift in attention, Brian began to slip back into his old ways of not studying and not making his education a priority.

In his English class, Brian and his peers were required to turn in a research paper at the end of the semester. Brian was a self-proclaimed horrible writer; he attributed his lack of grammar and overall writing skills to the fact that his high school English teachers never stressed the importance of formal writing.

A few days after handing them in, Brian and his classmates received their graded research papers. Brian began to look over his paper and he noticed a note that read, "Come and see me after class." *Oh no, this can't be good,* Brian thought to himself. Brian spent the whole class period wondering what he did wrong and how he would get himself out of whatever situation he was in.

After class was dismissed, Brian walked up to Professor Bisby with a look of sheer terror on his face. As Brian approached her, Professor Bisby asked a simple question: "Did you read this paper?"

"No I didn't" Brian replied. Taken aback by his honest response, his instructor paused before retorting back. "I thought so, because *this is the worst paper I have ever read* since I have been in this profession! I am in awe that you have made it this far in your education with your writing skills, or should I say lack of. I do not feel as though you should be in college. Let me be clear: IF you write another paper like this, I will see that you never receive a degree from the University of Principles!"

Brian could not believe that his professor would say something so harsh. Brian took a long walk after class; he was in shock and devastated by his instructor's words. When he arrived to his empty dorm room, Brian broke down and cried all of the tears that he had kept hidden during his walk home. Not only was he not doing well in English, his relapse back to his old ways seemed to be a common theme throughout all of his courses.

* * *

Brian's thoughts frequently wandered as he sat in his college classes. One day, while daydreaming during History class, Brian had an unusual feeling; he saw a flash, followed by an overall brightness in the room. At that moment, it seemed like no one was in the room but Brian and his professor. At one point Brian thought someone was speaking to him; the voice proclaimed a message that Brian would never forget:

"Your purpose in life is to reach people and empower them to be great."

Brian answered this voice and said, "Who is this?" No response. At that moment, Brian thought he was crazy because he heard a voice. It didn't take Brian long to forgot about the whole incident.

* * *

The semester came to an end and Brian went home waiting for his grades to come out. A couple of days before Christmas, his grades came in. Brian ran to the mailbox and found the envelope he had been anticipating; after opening it up, he read, for the second time, that he had not maintained a 2.0 grade point average.

Assuming that the outcome would be different this time, Brian traveled back to the University of Principles when the break was over. However, he was met with the same fate that he had experienced the previous year.

Brian once again had to call his parents and tell them the bad news. Lovingly and without asking any questions, Brian's mother sent him a plane ticket to come home. The thing that hurt Brian the most was knowing that his mother and father had worked so hard to put him through school yet he was unable to uphold his end of the deal. During his plane ride home, Brian spent a lot of time reflecting on his experiences and choices up to this point in his life.

Brian felt that the University of Principles served its purpose; along with meeting loyal friends, Brian came to the conclusion that he was not taking his education seriously and that he needed to reevaluate his life. For the first time, he realized that life is like a marathon: He couldn't just sprint a few times and expect to succeed. Rather, he had to prepare himself for the long distance. If he was going to finish his undergraduate degree, Brian would have to run at a steady pace to the finish line, regardless of the hurdles that would inevitably appear on his way.

WHAT DO YOU WANT OUT OF LIFE?

BRIAN'S TRANSITION YEARS

After failing out of school for the second time in two years, continuing his education was the furthest thing from Brian's mind. While he was discouraged and felt like a failure, deep down Brian knew that he needed to start envisioning a future for himself.

Chapter Seven: What Do You Want Out Of Life?

It was time to go back to school and Mr. and Mrs. Anderson sat down with Brian to discuss their son's plans for the upcoming semester. Mr. Anderson began the conversation by asking his son a simple question: "Do you *want* to go back to school?" After a brief hesitation, Brian finally mustered up a response. "No, it is time for me to make some changes in my life and that means I can't go back Texas."

"Are you sure that is a good idea, sweetie?" Mrs. Anderson asked lovingly of her son. "There is nothing more important than a quality education. I know you are not feeling like your best self right now, but I do not want you to make a decision that you will regret for the rest of your life."

"This is the best thing for me, mom. I know it is," Brian replied. Without even looking in her direction, Brian could sense the concern and sadness in his mother's voice.

The following day, Brian had to face what seemed like the most difficult and embarrassing situation of his entire life: telling his boys that he would not be joining them for the upcoming semester. For almost a month,

Brian had been dreading the idea of making this phone call. Although the decision was his and his alone, he wished that someone other than himself could inform his friends that he would not be returning to the University of Principles.

After three rings, Brian was greeted by a familiar voice. "What's up? This is Jason." "Yo man, it's me. I'm going to make this short. I am not coming back to school."

Jason paused for a minute before laughing at the absurdity of his friend's announcement. "Man, stop playing. What time do I need to come and pick you up from airport?" "I wish I was playing but I can't come back, man." At that moment, Jason realized that his friend was not joking around. "Everyone is looking for you, brother. You can't just leave us like that. What's going on, man?" Jason replied.

"This has been a tough decision to make but I realized that coming back to school would be a big mistake. Man, you know I wasn't doing well. I wasn't studying and, honestly, I don't really feel like going through the stress of going to school right now. I need to figure out what I want in life!" Brian replied.

Brian knew that his friends were feeling like he was letting them down. However, deep down Brian knew that he was making the right decision. Although he was unaware of it at the time, taking time off from his academic studies would be a defining moment in his life.

* * *

Brian quickly became bored by his new daily routine, which consisted of sleeping in, eating, napping, and watching television for the majority of the day. Since all of his friends were away at college for the spring semester, Brian's social life in Alabama was nonexistent. As a result, Brian had plenty of time to reflect on his short-term and long-term goals for himself.

One Friday afternoon in late August, Mrs. James, the Anderson's neighbor, spotted Brian as he walked to the mailbox. Mrs. James treated the youngster as if he was her own son. Brian, too, thought of his neighbor as a second mother figure in his life. As Brian walked up the driveway carrying his family's mail in both hands, Mrs. James began the interrogation. "Why are you not in school this semester?" she shouted from across the street. "My grades were not good and so I decided that I needed a break from the school scene. I'll probably try the 'school thing' again in the Fall."

Known for her need to lovingly speak her mind, Brian's neighbor asked a well-thought out follow-up question. "Are you going to work while you are waiting to go back?" "I don't know, Mrs. James. I haven't really thought about it." Brian replied.

The following day, Mrs. James invited Brian over to her house for lunch. The conversation consisted of a variety of topics: updates on their families, the weather, and current events (the anticipated "end of the world" due to the Y2K computer situation, the latest video games to be released, and so on.) After discussing their families' plans for the Labor Day weekend, Mrs. James's disposition changed from lighthearted to serious. At that moment, Brian knew that it was time for "the talk" about his future.

"Brian, tomorrow morning you need to wake up early and go find a job. You WILL NOT come back home without one. Do you hear me?" "Yes, ma'am," Brian replied. The following day Brian woke up at 7A.M. and set out on his quest of finding a job.

Aaron was an acquaintance of Brian who worked as a manager at Roger's, a local grocery store. Brian knew that Roger's was an obvious first stop. Brian walked into the store and asked a young man working in the produce section if he could speak with Aaron. The guy nodded and walked through a door labeled *Employees Only.*

After a brief conversation, Aaron offered Brian a part time position working in the seafood department of the grocery store. Sure, cleaning and peeling shrimp and making party platters would not be the most glorious job, but it was a job nonetheless. By 9am Brian walked out of Roger's with a huge sense of accomplishment.

Brian knew the first thing he had to do when he got back from his adventure. He walked over to Mrs. James's house to tell her his good news. "I got a job!" Brian exclaimed. Mrs. James gave Brian a congratulatory smile as she held him in a long embrace. Mrs. James's hug and gentle smile seemed to say *I am so proud of you. You did it!* without her even saying a word.

For the first time in a very long time, Brian felt pride in himself. He felt good about his accomplishment because he did not fail at this task like he typically did in the past. For the first time Brian did not have to think about school. He was excited to focus on work while thinking about his next move.

* * *

Brian's first six months of working at the grocery store came and went. He was working twenty-five hours a week at minimum wage. While walking home from work one afternoon, Brian realized that he wanted to work more hours and for better pay.

Mr. Anderson worked at the cafeteria for a large and well-known, locally as well as nationally, company. He suggested to Brian that he come out there and work with him. The decision to work with his dad was a no brainer. Brian would have weekends off and the pay would be significantly better than that of his current job.

Mr. Anderson's boss, Mrs. Flowers, thought very highly of Brian's father. As a result, she did him a favor and set up an interview with his son for the following day. As with his interview at Rogers, Brian went to the interview and was hired on the spot. Although Brian had no idea what position he was just hired for, he was excited to work with his dad every day.

After accepting the position, Mrs. Flowers explained that Brian would be working in the deli line. This job would consist of preparing the meats, breads, and toppings (lettuce, tomato, onion, to name a few) and then making the sandwiches "to order" as customers walked through the deli line during the lunch rush.

Brian had mixed feelings about working in the cafeteria with his father. For one, he knew he had to live up to his father's standards of highly effective work standards. Mr. Anderson believed in perfection in the workplace and, as a young carefree adolescent, this was not Brian's idea of a good time. Although Brian's dad held his son to the same standards that he expected the rest of his coworkers to adhere to, Brian quickly realized that this was a good thing. Brian knew that his father would reprimand him before Mrs. Flowers had a chance to take disciplinary action. Additionally, Brian had to be at work by five-thirty every weekday morning. At first, Brian despised the idea of waking up before sunrise. However, the early morning wake-ups became much more bearable when Brian realized that ending his work day by two-thirty in the afternoon left plenty of daylight time to hang out with his college friends.

* * *

One day, Brian and his boss got into an argument about his performance. As part of his job, one of Brian's duties was to set up caterings for big meetings. Prior to each meeting, Mrs. Flower would give Brian a list of all the items requested for the meeting. Usually these meetings would ask for breakfast food items and juice. Although the customers would typically request breakfast items, such as orange juice and pastries, it was important for Brian to get the orders right for these important meetings.

On this particular Monday, Mrs. Flowers accused Brian of failing to prepare all of the items needed for a large catering event. Mrs. Flowers called Brian into the office and started yelling at him for forgetting to order bagels and cream cheese. Brian realized that he did, in fact, forget to order these items. However, Brian did not feel as though his mistake was a valid excuse for being talked down to by his boss. As a loyal and respected employee, he believed that he deserved better.

Frustrated and angry, Brian went home and told his mom that he was going to quit his job the following day. As always, Mrs. Anderson had a different outlook on this situation. She advised her son to calm down and to speak with his boss after he had time to rationally reflect on the day's events.

The following day, Brian went into work and explained to Mrs. Flowers that how she spoke to him was not right. He apologized for forgetting to order the bagels and cream cheese and ensured his boss that he would double check the orders before submitting them next time. Mrs. Flower's appreciated the fact that Brian came to her to express his feelings in a calm and respectful manner. She apologized for offending Brian with her words and harsh tone.

Brian learned the importance of reflection rather than overreaction. He realized that it was more beneficial to be proactive, rather than reactive, when dealing with adult issues in a mature manner.

* * *

After one year of working at both the grocery store and cafeteria, Brian decided that the time was right for him to go back to school. Brian quit his job at Rogers and began taking night classes at a nearby Huntington Community College, a community college located in Brian's town. Between going to class and focusing on his studies, Brian started hanging out with some of the guys in his night classes. Since Brian no longer had to work at the grocery store on the weekends, he had plenty of time to go out and socialize with his new friends.

Everything was beginning to fall into place for Brian. He was keeping his grades up at school, gaining respect at his job, and enjoying the time spent with his new group of friends.

To add to his newfound happiness, Brian found a new hobby that incorporated his love of music; becoming a disc jockey at local clubs. Brian saved his money and bought the essential DJ equipment; two record players and a mixer. While Brian was buying records at a record store one day, he overheard a conversation between a customer and an employee of the store. The customer was looking for high-quality equipment for him and his crew to utilize during their upcoming club appearances.

Never one to miss an opportunity to network, Brian walked over to speak with the young disc jockey. "Hey, I'm Brian. I overheard you talking about having a DJ crew and I was wondering if I could come meet your guys sometime." "Hey, what's up, my name is Jamal. Sure, here's my address. My boys and I are getting together tonight to make sure we're ready for our upcoming club appearance. Feel free to stop by."

Brian decided to take Jamal up on his offer. Later on that night, Brian packed up his new equipment and latest hits records and drove over to Jamal's house. The guys loved Brian and all agreed that he would be a great addition to their crew. For the next few weeks, Brian and his new DJ friends began to hang out and work on their music skills on a daily basis.

About a month later, Jamal got a call from a local club. They offered him and his crew a five-hour time slot every Saturday night at a local club. This was the break the young men had been waiting for. Every weekend thereafter, Brian spent his Saturday nights in the club until five in the morning.

* * *

One Sunday morning in the beginning of April, Mrs. Anderson was in the kitchen cooking breakfast as Brian struggled to wake up from his long night out at the club. Mrs. Anderson looked at Brian and asked, *"What do you want out of life?"* With a puzzling look on his face, Brian responded. "Mom, I don't know. I'm having fun and, to be honest, that is all I really care about right now. Isn't that enough?"

"At some point, hopefully sooner rather than later, you will realize that your life cannot revolve around 'fun' forever. When you decide that the time is right to focus on other endeavors, you may be met with resistance from your friends. Although it will be difficult, always remember that others may not want or appreciate the opportunities you are given throughout your life." Brian did not think much of his mother's words of wisdom, as he truly believed that she was unable to relate to the younger generation.

* * *

It was about to be fall again and Brian was ready to go back to school full-time. So, he went to his parents and asked them if he could quit work and focus on school. Mrs. Anderson tried with all her might to hide her delight in her son's much needed awakening. Mr. and Mrs. Anderson went into the living room to deliberate on Brian's request. When they came back to the kitchen, it was Mr. Anderson's turn to address his son.

"Your mom and I are very proud of you and all that you have accomplished thus far in your life. We agree that the time is right for you to focus on your education. We are very pleased that you came to this realization on your own. As always, we will continue to support you in accomplishing your goals." "Thank you, mom and dad! I know that I haven't always made it easy for you to accept my decisions and path in life, but I do not know what I would do without your support. I will not let you down this time, I promise." Brian began to feel confident that he was on the right path in his life.

A few days later, Brian went and told his friends that he was going to focus on his education. One of the guys said to him, *"What are you going to do, go to school for the rest of your life?"* Brian had flashbacks of his conversation with his mother in the kitchen a few months prior. Brian recalled what his mom meant when she said that he his friends would not always appreciate his choices in his life.

Brian was beginning to appreciate the wisdom passed on to him by his parents.

FACING YOUR GREATEST FEARS

BRIAN'S...

After getting a glimpse of how the real world works, Brian was ready to face his biggest fear: going back to school full-time. Brian understood that he must take advantage of this second chance if he was going to make a better life for himself.

Chapter Eight: Facing Your Greatest Fears

Located five minutes from his parents' house in Alabama, Brian was confident that the University of Adversity would be a great fit for him. After all, he did not have a single friend at this school to distract him from his studies. Brian knew that this time *had* to be different, especially because he was running out of opportunities to earn his college degree.

The week before the start of classes, Brian met with Ms. Thomas, the advisor for the University of Adversity's Education Department. Together, they designed a plan for Brian to earn his teaching degree.

Ms. Thomas explained the university's expectations and requirements for each of its teacher candidates. First, each interested student must apply and be accepted into the teacher preparation Program. Once accepted, they must maintain an overall GPA of 3.0.

"Mr. Anderson, as I am sure you are aware, the University of Adversity's College of Education is extremely competitive. I have reviewed your transcript from your previous university and see that you had a 2.2 GPA. Unfortunately, you do not qualify for acceptance into the College of Education at this time." Ms. Thomas took a long breath before continuing. "I do believe, however, that it is possible for you to get into the program if you put forth your best effort in order to achieve a 2.75 GPA."

"I *can* and *will* do it!" Brian proclaimed. The young man was determined to speak his words into existence. Brian knew that this time would be different. Knowing that he was taking a huge risk, Brian signed up for elective courses that he would need *if* he made it into the university's teaching program.

Since Brian's mother and father paid for his education at the University of Principles, Brian felt that it was his turn to take financial responsibility for his education. He filled out all of the paperwork necessary to take out loans for his studies. Now that he was paying for his own college tuition, Brian needed to find a way to lessen his financial burden. Through regular visits to chat with the ladies in the University of Adversity's financial aid office, Brian found out about a work study opportunity at a nearby Boys & Girls Club. With this program, he would be able to pay off a huge chunk of his tuition by helping local kids with their homework. He happily accepted this position.

* * *

Year One, Semester One

Brian was adjusting well to life at the University of Adversity. In addition to turning in all of his assignments on time and studying for every test, he maintained either a "B" or "C" average in three out of his four classes.

His political science class, however, was a completely different story. Brian believed that his professor for his political science class, Professor. Henson, treated his students as if they were all going to work on political campaigns or run for a public office. Since his goal was to make it into the College of Education, these professions were not even on Brian's radar. Not surprisingly, Brian was not doing well in this class and began slipping back into his old ways once again. Fearing that a failing grade would mess up his prospect of getting into the University of Adversity's College of Education, Brian withdrew from the course early in the semester.

Since his studies were going relatively well, Brian began spending more and more time with the youth at the Boys and Girls Club. Every evening after his work study program, Brian joined several other college students in working with thirteen to fifteen-year-old young men who signed up for an afterschool mentoring program. Brian used his passion for helping others to teach his mentees coping mechanisms for dealing with peer pressure and making good decisions. Brian also volunteered to be the boys' basketball coach at the club.

One afternoon, a distressed group of girls told the director of the Boys and Girls Club that their friend's purse was stolen from the girls' locker room while they were playing volleyball. After hearing about the theft, Brian found out that the culprit was a member of his basketball team. He decided that he needed to take the matter into his own hands. Brian told the Director that he did not want the boy kicked off of the team, but that should be suspended from playing in at least one game. Since the teenager eventually admitted to taking the young girl's purse, the Director did not take Brian's suggestion into consideration. Instead, he decided to let the boy stay on the team without repercussions.

Brian decided to quit coaching the basketball team immediately after this confrontation. Brian believed that the only reason the boy confessed was because he was caught. "Would he have felt remorse if he was never caught for his malicious act?" Brian pondered.

Brian was deeply disturbed by this entire situation. He realized that working with youth was his calling in life. More specifically, he realized that shaping the moral character of troubled and misguided teens, such as the one he encountered at the Boys and Girls Club, was part of God's plan for him.

Brian finished his first semester at the University of Adversity with two "B"s and one "C." For the first time, he did not have to run to the mailbox to intercept his grades before his parents arrived home from work.

After viewing his grades, Brian's parents were ecstatic and extremely proud of their son. That night, Brian and his parents went out to dinner to celebrate his academic success.

Brian's parents could see that their son was finally taking his education seriously. However, they continued to hold their breath and pray that this turn-around would not be temporary.

While Brian was beginning to get his life together, his cousin, George, was not excelling academically at the university he was attending in Wisconsin. As a result, George's father felt that it was best for his son to move back to Alabama to finish his college education. As his life-long "partner-in-crime," Brian was thrilled that his cousin would soon be joining him at the University of Adversity.

Several days after receiving the good (according to Brian) news about his cousin, Brian brought his report card to Mrs. James' house. After viewing the document, she told Brian that his grades were *good*, but she wanted him to bring his "C" up. She was proud of the progress that the young man had made since his return to Alabama. However, she also recognized Brian's capability to achieve even greater academic success.

Brian felt that his neighbor's expectations were unreasonably high. "Could I really achieve a "B" in every class next semester?" he asked of himself silently. Brian did not know the answer to this question. Even so, the young man was grateful for the high level of belief that Mrs. James had in him.

On his way out of his neighbor's house, Mrs. James gave Brian a blunt yet tender reality check. "If you don't continue to keep your grades up, I will make sure that George goes back to the North!" As ridiculous as the threat sounded, Brian knew that Mrs. James meant every word that came out of her mouth. Brian did not want his favorite cousin to leave so he knew that his grades would have to be good.

* * *

Year One, Semester Two

Most of the friends Brian had made thus far were seniors at the school. As a result, they were able to advise him about which professors were acceptable to them and the ones to stay far, far, away from. Brian registered to take four education classes that were open to all students, not just students who were accepted into the education program.

Brian signed up for two classes that centered on the research and philosophies of well-known theorists in the world of education. Prior to taking this course, Brian thought that he already had a good grasp on the connections between teaching and learning. Brian already knew that above all, educators must be able to relate to their pupils. Once that student-teacher relationship is built, students will easily retain *all* of the knowledge given to them by their teachers. It was that simple. As the class clown during his school years, Brian knew that he could easily build relationships with his future students through the use of humor.

At the beginning of the semester, Brian was not convinced that learning about the educational philosophies of others would be useful to him and his future students. However, he soon realized that there was more to being a teacher than he had previously thought. Through his study of Howard Gardner, Brian realized that not all individuals learned the same way as he did. Although Brian benefitted from the use of pictures, texts, and visual models, others retained information through the use of songs, poems, and information read aloud to them. Brian was amazed that there were so many different learning styles and strategies.

Through his educational technology course, Brian learned about innovative media sources that would be useful in his future classroom(s). Brian was introduced to the basics of integrating video clips and PowerPoint presentations into daily instruction. By far, this was

Brian's favorite class of the semester. Through his interactions with the young kids and teenagers at the Boys and Girls Club, Brian realized how big of a role technology played in their everyday lives. He was excited to bring the academic content alive and to build relationships with his students through his newfound technological skills.

Throughout Brian's class about exceptional learners, Brian was introduced to characteristics of common learning disabilities and best practice approaches to effectively teach students with a wide range of learning, emotional, and behavioral needs. This class brought back flashbacks of Brian's elementary, middle, and high school years. One situation vividly stood out in Brian's mind: his struggle while learning to read. In the third grade, Brian was reading on a first grade level. He remembered the anxiety he had felt when he was unable to read third grade-level reading passages as well as the answer choices on his multiple choice tests. Brian also remembered the frustration of feeling like his teacher did not care about him or his academic success.

Now, as a college student, Brian looked back at his early years and wondered if he had a learning disability. He wondered how different his school experiences would have been if one, just one, teacher had realized how much Brian was struggling to keep a passing grade in the majority of his classes. Brian was convinced that if some of the strategies covered in this class were used by his own teachers, he may have struggled less and achieved greater academic success.

The semester came to a close and, sure enough, Brian raised his grades to straight "B"s. Mr. and Mrs. Anderson, as well as Mrs. James, realized that Brian was serious about achieving long-term academic success. For the first time, Brian's parents allowed their son to live at home and enjoy a work-free summer.

* * *

Year Two, Semester One

Still unable to apply for the University of Adversity's Teacher Education Program, Brian signed up for every history course that would count toward his degree plan. All three of Brian's classes (U.S. History, World Religion, and History of the South) were taught by an instructor named Professor Jones. Mr. Jones' teaching style captivated Brian's interest in the social sciences. Through his lectures, Professor Jones treated history like a free-flowing story. He consistently found real-life connections between the information being studied and current events. No matter the topic, Professor Jones never failed to make history come alive without the use of a single textbook.

One day after class, Professor Jones asked Brian to follow him to his office. "What did I do wrong?" Brian thought to himself as he walked down the hall and sat down across from his instructor.

"Brian, do you like history?" inquired Mr. Jones. "Yes, I guess so. But only the way you teach it," Brian replied.

"Well, thank you for the compliment. Let me get straight to the point. Have you ever thought about pursuing a career as a historian?" Brian looked around to see if his professor was in fact talking to him. Brian, confused as to why he was being asked this question, replied after a brief moment of silence. "I don't think that I would make a good historian, sir. Historians have to be able to read and write well. Neither of those things are my strengths."

"Do not sell yourself short, Brian. I always enjoy reading your papers. When I read them, it's like reading about a magical journey through the past. You always have something special to say. You are correct … your grammar is far from amazing. However, those are skills that you can continue to work on."

Before leaving the office, Brian promised his professor that he would consider a career in the field of history as well as a switch from an education to history college degree.

Brian's drive home from class seemed to take an hour. He could not wait to tell his parents that the

University of Adversity's best professor (in his opinion) thought that he had the qualities of a historian.

For the first time that he could remember, a teacher believed in him. This was the greatest day of Brian's life thus far.

Brian spent the entire weekend mulling over his options. If he continued to pursue a degree in teaching, Brian would have to apply for the university's Teacher Education Program in the fall, finish his education courses as well as student teaching, and graduate the following spring. If he changed his major to pursue a degree in history, Brian would need to take, at most, two more semesters of classes. Eager to graduate, Brian made the decision to change his major.

Brian arrived at Professor Jones' office bright and early on Monday morning. "I thought about our talk last week and I want to change my major from education to history," Brian confidently proclaimed. Professor Jones had a big smile on his face because he knew that Brian would make a great historian someday. The professor helped his student to fill out the paperwork needed to change his major.

After reviewing the courses that Brian had already taken, Professor Jones found that most of his education courses could be used as electives toward his history degree. In addition to the change in major, Professor Jones recommended that Brian pursue a minor in political science in order for him to graduate the coming May.

After officially changing his Major and Minor at the University of Adversity's Office of Admissions, Brian called his mother to tell her about his change in major and upcoming graduation. Mrs. Anderson began to cry tears of joy. As Brian's greatest cheerleader, she was ecstatic that all of his hard work was finally paying off.

Year Two, Semester Two

Brian's final semester at the University of Adversity flew by. Now that he was able to see "the light at the end of the tunnel," he regularly attended his classes and studied for each of his tests.

The day grades came out, Brian walked to the mailbox and found an envelope with his name on it: BRIAN ANDERSON. Brian knew that the contents of this envelope would signify whether or not he would become a graduate of the University of Adversity in ten days.

Upon opening the envelope and viewing the document that was inside, Brian broke down and cried. Then it hit him like a bolt of lightning; a couple of years ago, he was being kicked out of college but now he would be a college graduate in less than two weeks.

Graduation day finally arrived. Not only were Brian and George graduating together, but graduation was scheduled during Mother's Day weekend. Brian knew that this special day was fate. He could think of no better present to give his mother than for her to witness her son, dressed in his cap and gown, walking across the stage to receive his diploma. She had sacrificed so much for Brian and he finally felt like he was giving her a return on her investment.

After failing out of his former college and getting rejected from the education program at the University of Adversity, Brian continued to face his greatest fear: failure. With the support of his parents and favorite teacher, Brian overcame these challenges and earned a Bachelor of Science in History with a minor in Political Science.

Taking Advantage of Opportunities

Brian's...

Brian was now a college graduate. As the end of summer drew near, Brian knew that it was time to make a decision on what his next step in life would be.

Chapter Nine: Taking Advantage of Opportunities

Brian graduated from college during a time when the job market as a whole was bleak. To make matters worse, the young man's lack of writing skills prevented him from applying for many entry-level positions.

"What in the world was I thinking? I'll *never* find a job that appreciates my history degree, especially with only a *Bachelor's* in it!" Brian frequently contemplated whether he made the right or wrong decision by changing when he changed his major. Surprisingly, Brian decided to go back to school. He wanted to pursue a teaching degree, just like he was trying to do in the first place.

Brian finished his first degree program at the University of Adversity with a 2.8 GPA. Because of this, he was able to apply for the university's Teacher Education Program. After being accepted into the program, he met with Mrs. Thomas once again. She advised Brian of the classes he needed to take in order to earn a Bachelor of Science in Secondary Education Social Sciences.

Much to his dismay, Brian was required to take a writing class. Professor Jim, the professor for this course, challenged Brian's writing skills by always demanding more from him. Although Brian knew that the quality of his writing was progressively improving each week, he was still receiving a "C" grade on every one of his papers.

Bothered by his lack of progress, Brian visited Professor Jim at his office one afternoon. "Professor, is there anything I can do to improve my writing? I am trying the best I know how to. Can you please give me some advice?" Professor Jim was impressed by Brian's eagerness to better himself academically. His advice was simple: read a variety of fiction and nonfiction texts to become familiar with the qualities of high-quality writing. Brian took his professor's advice seriously. In addition to reading one novel based on the battles of the Civil War, Brian read a different peer-reviewed journal article each week. By the end of the semester, Brian was receiving "A"s and "B"s on all of his assignments for Professor Jim's class. Now Brian felt that he was in control of his education and it felt great.

After finishing all of his coursework for the University of Adversity's Teacher Education Program, Brian was ready to begin student teaching. His placement was at Parkman High School, which was great because it was close to his home. The student teaching component of this program was sixteen weeks long.

On the first day of student teaching, Brian drove to Parkman High School and met his cooperating teacher, Mrs. Ruby. Mrs. Ruby had been a teacher for about fifteen years. For the first several weeks, Brian was to observe or "shadow" her. After getting to know the students and classroom structure, Mrs. Ruby would allow Brian to teach classes in a gradual fashion. For example, after four weeks of shadowing Mrs. Ruby, Brian would teach one class during Week 5, two classes during Week 6, and so on. This would continue until Brian was teaching by himself for three whole weeks. At least once a week, Mrs. Ruby and Brian were required to have a meeting in which Mrs. Ruby would give her student teaching candidate some guidance on his teaching.

Yet, once again, Brian's life did not seem to go right. After a month of shadowing Mrs. Ruby, the school made a sudden shift when an administrator at the school abruptly retired. Since she had always wanted to be an administrator, Mrs. Ruby was taken out of the classroom and given the title of "Assistant Principal."

When Brian first heard the news, he was angry. He thought that this was the school's way of making sure he failed his student teaching placement. Although he did not feel that he was ready to become the main teacher, he began to surround himself with positive thoughts. "You have the determination of a lion" was his favorite mantra that he repeated whenever his classroom management techniques or lessons did not go as planned.

Brian did a fantastic job of teaching and the students loved his teaching style. Although difficult at times, this experience was a great challenge with great rewards.

Brian learned that when presented with a sudden opportunity you must take advantage of it and roll up your sleeves. He had to do what was necessary to make success happen. As a result, Brian earned a Bachelor of Science in Secondary Education Social Sciences at the University of Adversity.

MAKING EXCELLENCE HAPPEN

A disheartened Brian spent his summer watching TV, reading outside, and hanging out with cousin. Once again, Brian found himself facing a challenge that he was not prepared to face.

Chapter Ten: Making Excellence Happen

Since he could not find a teaching job, Brian believed that going back to school to complete his Master's degree was his best option. Brian began to research graduate programs at several local universities. During this time, Brian ran into yet another roadblock; in order to apply to the majority of graduate schools, he would need to pass the Graduate Record Examination, or GRE. The GRE, he was told, was an extremely difficult standardized assessment.

Brian thought that his struggles with taking standardized tests were over. He was not certain that going back to school was even worth it, especially if he would still end up jobless in the end.

While at the barbershop one afternoon, Brian vented about his dilemma to his barber. One of the patrons overheard this conversation and suggested that Brian apply to online universities because many of these schools did not require the GRE in order to be accepted. He suggested an online school called the University of Purpose. Brian went online and searched for Master's programs in history at the University of Purpose. Luckily, they had the exact program that Brian was looking for and, sure enough, the GRE was not a requirement. There was only one catch: if accepted, Brian would have to maintain an average of at least a 3.0 GPA.

Brian applied to the University of Purpose and was accepted into their Masters in History program the following day. Brian finally felt good about himself and was looking forward to studying subjects that he enjoyed. Brian took two history courses during his first semester of graduate school and received an "A" in one class and a "B" in the other. Brian had not experienced this kind of success in school before and it gave him the confidence he needed to get through the history program.

After his first semester at the University of Purpose, Brian took one class while working part-time at a General Education Development (GED) center. This GED center provided free online preparation classes to low-income members of the community who never finished their high school education and, as a result, did not earn a high school diploma. After taking the course, students would take the GED in hopes of earning a high school equivalency certificate.

At the center, Brian's responsibilities included monitoring the students as well as providing help and clarification as needed. Even with the addition of his part-time job, Brian was able to earn a "B" in his second-semester graduate course.

At the beginning of his second year at the University of Purpose, Emily asked Brian to move to Delaware. Brian hesitated before making a decision. Not only did his cousin and parents live in Alabama, but Brian had begun to make some genuine friends. Brian told Emily that he would think about it and get back to her later (which, in this situation, meant never.)

Three months later, Emily called Brian to follow up on their previous conversation about the possibility of him moving to Delaware. Emily, always the rational and practical sibling, expressed her feelings to her brother. "You need a fresh start in your life," she began, "and moving up here would be a big help to us; transporting the kids to all of their afterschool activities and events is becoming a huge struggle." Brian paused for a minute before responding. "Let me think about it and I will give you an answer soon."

Each day Brian prayed over the idea of moving to Delaware. While getting ready for work one morning in the beginning of May, Brian felt God's presence; *God was telling him to leave Alabama and make the move to Delaware.*

Still hesitant, Brian woke up the next morning and once again prayed his morning prayers. "Please, God. Send me a sign that I am making the right decision. Show me that I am doing what is best for me and my life."

Several hours later, Brian received a phone call from Carla, his coworker, who was currently the sitting president of the entire GED education program. "Hey

Brian, do you have a minute to talk?" asked the voice on the other end. "Yea, what's going on?" Brian could tell from the tone in Carla's voice that she was not about to give him good news. "They finally hired a permanent president for the program. So, I have to move back into your position. I hate that I have to be the one to tell you this."

Brian went completely silent. He was speechless. Assuming that her coworker was upset, Carla tried to comfort him. "I am very sorry that this is happening. Are you okay?" Brian began to jump up and down with tears of joy because he received the answer he was waiting for. *This was the sign from God that he had been praying about.* "Yes! Yes I am! Thank you for calling me!" After the call ended, Brian was sure that his coworker was confused as to why he was excited about losing his job.

Brian immediately called his sister and told her the good news. "I will be coming up to Delaware at the end of month! Isn't that great?" Emily was as elated, if not more, as her brother. When moving day arrived, Brian and George packed up Brian's SUV and made the trip to Delaware.

During his first week in Delaware, Brian received some disturbing news from his cousin George. George's father, who was Mrs. Anderson's oldest brother and Brian's Uncle Phil, was in the hospital in critical condition due to complications from COPD. Although he had been suffering from COPD for many years, his sickness took a sudden turn for the worst.

One week later, Emily and Brian received the phone call that they had been dreading: Uncle Phil had passed away early that morning. This news was a devastating blow to Brian because his Uncle Phil meant a lot to him. All of his life, Brian had done his best to follow in his uncle's footsteps. His uncle had been an elementary school teacher, and Brian would always listen to his stories about his students, coworkers, and overall experience working in an elementary school setting for hours at a time. Brian had no doubt in his mind that his uncle was well-liked by his students; after all, in Brian's eyes, Uncle Phil was the "cool uncle." As a result, Brian's goal in life was to be a teacher just like his Uncle Phil.

Brian and Emily flew to Alabama to attend their uncle's funeral. Once again, Brian had a difficult decision to make. Although he wanted to stay in Alabama to be with his cousin, he knew that his sister needed him in Delaware. Brian decided to continue to help out his sister and her family.

Despite his uncle's unanticipated death, Brian found time to focus on his Pre-Civil War online summer course at the University of Principles. He knew that no matter what, he needed to stay focused on his studies so that his grades would not slip. Brian's "A" at the end of the semester proved that his hard work had paid off.

At the end of the summer semester, Brian had three classes left before he would write his dreaded thesis paper. Brian intentionally saved these classes for last due to the amount of writing involved in all of them. As the time to take his final courses approached, Brian became frustrated thinking about the amount of work that was still ahead of him.

Brian had heard that every single one of these classes had a research paper due at the end of the semester. Because of this, Brian planned to take one class per semester. However, his plans changed after he received a bit of coaching from his sister. "Why don't you think about taking two classes this semester?" Emily asked. "Don't you want to finish your degree sooner rather than later?" Brian knew that his sister was making a good point, but he was hesitant about writing two research papers in one semester due to his weak writing skills. However, the young man knew it was time for him to stop making excuses. Brian hesitantly signed up for *two* of his remaining writing-intensive courses.

At the end of August, Brian went online to review the syllabus for each of his classes. Sure enough, both of the classes required a final paper. Brian felt defeated before his classes even started. Brian's head was filled with negative thoughts about himself and his future. "I can't believe I listened to my sister. I am going to flunk both of my classes. So long, graduation!" After pouting for several hours, Brian picked himself up and began to work on his first assignment for both of his classes.

One morning in October, Brian woke up with a throbbing pain in his right eye, which was the eye in which Brian wore a contact due to a condition known as **Keratoconus**. Something felt unusual about the pain he was currently feeling and Brian was sure that he was not experiencing an ordinary eye infection. He got dressed and took himself to the local medical clinic to get his eye checked out.

Brian sat in the waiting room of the medical clinic for less than ten minutes before his name was called. Dr. Brown, the doctor on site, looked at Brian's right eye. "You have some sort of infection in your right eye. You'll need to keep your contact out for the next seven days. Also, due to your diagnoses of **Keratoconus**, I would highly recommend making an appointment with your eye doctor as soon as possible." Brian could not believe the news he was receiving from Dr. Brown. Without his contact, he would not be able to read his textbooks or complete his many assignments. Although he was freaking out on the inside, Brian knew that he needed to stay calm until he knew exactly what was going on with his eye. Luckily, due to an appointment cancellation, Brian was able to set up an appointment with his eye doctor for the following day.

The next day, Brian arrived thirty minutes early for his appointment with his optometrist, Dr. Kevin. After conducting a thorough eye exam, Dr. Kevin reviewed the results with his patient. "Brian, the good news is that your eye exam did not show anything out of the ordinary with your right eye. However, the findings did show some abnormalities in your left eye due to the Keratoconus. We will make an appointment for you to see an ophthalmologist for your left eye."

Dr. Kevin referred Brian to his colleague, Dr. Jeffrey. Dr. Jeffrey was an ophthalmologist, which meant that he was certified to diagnose and treat specific eye diseases as well as perform necessary eye surgeries. Dr. Kevin's office set up an appointment for Brian to see Dr. Jeffrey the following week.

Brian did not expect much from his appointment with Dr. Jeffrey. However, he could not have been more wrong. For the first time in his life, Brian was given a detailed description of his rare eye condition. "Most people's retinas have a U-shape, which only lets in the necessary light. For individuals with Keratoconus, however, their retinas are like a cone, which lets in all light, necessary as well as unnecessary. As a result, many people with your condition become blind over a period of time."

Dr. Jeffrey then explained that since he was of a young age, Brian would be the perfect candidate for a cornea transplant. With this transplant, Brian would (hopefully) be able to see clearly for the first time in a very long time. At the end of his visit with Dr. Jeffrey, Brian set up an appointment in January for his cornea transplant.

* * *

Each year on Thanksgiving, Emily cooked a big turkey dinner for her family. This year, Brian convinced George to come up to visit. Brian hoped that this trip would help keep George's mind off of his father's passing. When the week of Thanksgiving arrived, Brian could barely stand the anticipation of his cousin's first trip to Delaware.

By the time George arrived in Delaware, Brian had four more weeks left in his fall semester. Although he wanted to spend as much time as he could with his cousin, he knew that he had to keep his focus on his schoolwork. At this time, however, Brian's eyesight was beginning to worsen. Despite his declining vision, Brian came up with a plan in which he would tackle the remaining assignments for both of his classes. First, he would focus on his four initial discussion posts. Next, Brian would begin writing his two research papers, one for each class. While working on his papers, Brian would reply to two of his classmates' discussion posts (two responses per post, which equaled eight responses in all.)

Brian knew that he had to finish up the semester strong, regardless of his limited eyesight. After some serious brainstorming, Brian found a way to connect his computer to his sister's brand new 73-inch television. Now, Brian was able to read his journal articles *and* see the words that he typed in his discussion posts and research papers.

Throughout the holiday weekend, Brian struggled to complete his assignments while George and the rest of his family sat upstairs sharing many laughs and quality time together. Brian was frustrated that he had to listen to his family having fun while he was downstairs struggling to write his two-hundred and fifty-word discussion posts.

Brian thought about emailing his professors for extensions on his assignments.

Then, Brian began having flashbacks of all of the obstacles he had faced and overcome along his educational journey thus far.

"This is not the time to give up," he told himself. Brian decided to work as hard as he could to finish his assignments. He completed all four discussion posts, as well as responses to his peers' posts, in three days. Completing these smaller assignments left Brian with three weeks to write his two research papers. With the aid of his sisters' television and an abundance of visual breaks, Brian read all of his articles and completed his two research papers with three days to spare.

The semester ended, and Brian achieved an "A" in one class and a "B" in the other. Although Brian was proud of his past accomplishments, nothing even came close to the pride he felt after receiving his grades for this challenging semester. Although Brian had been frustrated with his sister for forcing him to take two classes, in the end he thanked her for pushing him beyond his comfort zone.

Under extreme circumstances, Brian overcame the unthinkable and made excellence happen.

* * *

January quickly approached and Brian had his cornea transplant in his left eye. Although the surgery went well and was free of complications, Brian spent the next two months in recovery. This meant he was unable to take part in many activities he enjoyed, such as play-wrestling with his nephew and binge-watching his favorite television programs. During the first month of his recovery period, Brian's mother came up to Delaware to help take care of her son.

In February, Brian scheduled a follow-up appointment with Dr. Jeffrey to see how well his left eye was healing. The doctor was impressed by the speed at which Brian's vision was becoming restored. "We must have found a great match for you! You are one of the lucky ones, because this is extremely rare."

Brian knew that he was being blessed. Yet again, he was reminded that he was on his way to making excellence happen.

In March, Brian began his last three-credit course before writing his thesis. For this class, Brian chose an 8-week elective course that centered on the process of writing a graduate-level thesis paper. Prior to taking this class, Brian was unaware that he lacked so many foundational writing skills. Over the 8-week period, Brian learned the basics of sentence and paragraph writing, how to pick a thesis topic, and how to use journal articles and many other scholarly resources to support the main idea or argument of a thesis paper. Brian was pleased that he had the opportunity to take this course prior to writing his thesis. Although his writing was still below average, he no longer feared the whole writing process.

In May, Brian began the process of writing his thesis paper. Brian made a vow to himself that he would do his best and not worry about the grade. Brian needed assistance with locating the peer-reviewed resources, so he reached out to a local university called the University of Scholars. Brian went online and found the phone number for the College of Women's Studies at the University of

Scholars. The Secretary of the college gave Brian the contact information for two of the college's professors that she believed could and would help him. Right away, Brian emailed both of the professors and hoped that at least one of them would write back to him. Since he was not a student at the university, he knew that this was a longshot and tried his best not to get his hopes up.

After over a week without a response, Brian was checking his emails one day when he noticed that a woman with a University of Scholar's email address had replied back to his email. She wrote, "Hello my name is Dr. Mary and I would love to help you in any way that I can! When is a good day for you to meet me at my office?" Elated that someone actually took the time to respond, Brian set up a date and time that worked for both Dr. Mary and himself.

Dr. Mary was a well-respected full-time professor at the University of Scholars. According to Dr. Mary, the best part of her job was helping students to reach and acknowledge their full potential as lifelong learners. Dr. Mary helped Brian to solidify the topic for his thesis paper. When Brian decided to write his thesis about the importance of African American women during the Women's Suffrage Movement, Dr. Mary was ready and willing to assist Brian with researching his topic.

While at the University of Purpose, each graduate student was assigned a professor who would read his or her thesis. Although all correspondence took place online or over the phone, each professor was responsible for making sure that their mentee(s) was/were meeting all of the deadlines listed in the syllabus. From the start, Brian did not receive a good vibe from his mentor. Brian was not sure if he was comparing his mentor to Dr. Mary, or if there really was something about her that he did not like.

Each month, Brian was required to turn in one chapter of his thesis to his mentor. After reviewing his submission, his mentor would give feedback on what he had written so far. Each time he submitted his assignment, Brian received the same feedback; according to his mentor, Brian's thesis did not answer a specific question or argue a specific point-of-view on his topic; rather, his paper was more of a biographical piece. This frustrated Brian. Since this was his first time writing a thesis he was not well-versed in all of the ins and outs of writing a thesis paper. Brian, however, refused to let his mentor's criticisms get in his way of achieving a graduate degree. Brian continued to have a positive outlook and prayed that his paper would turn out okay.

Two weeks before the end of class, Brian submitted the rough draft of his thesis paper. Brian had worked long hours researching his topic and writing his paper; hopefully, this hard work would work in his favor. Although his mentor had done nothing but criticize Brian's writing skills thus far, Brian was hoping that she would have a change of heart this time around.

The next morning, Brian woke up early and logged onto his computer to see if his professor had read and provided feedback on his rough draft. Sure enough, Brian received an email notification to let him know that his mentor had reviewed and commented on his submission. Before looking at his mentor's comments, Brian took a deep breath and hoped for the best.

His mentor's comments included the following: "The format of your paper is completely wrong. You did not, in any way, incorporate any of my past recommendations. Therefore, it is in your best interest to rewrite your paper if you wish to receive a passing grade on your thesis argument. Don't forget, your final draft is due next Friday."

Brian's spirit was completely shattered. Not only had his mentor torn his paper apart, Brian only had five days left until his final thesis was due. Brian was so hurt that he could not think straight for the entire day. In his mind, Brian repeated the same question over and over again: "How could this happen to me?"

After spending the majority of the day crying and lying in his bed, Brian eventually got himself out of bed, walked up the stairs to the kitchen, and explained his predicament to his sister. Although he spoke in a calm manner, Emily could tell that her brother was emotionally overwhelmed. She told him to take a day off and to try to revamp his paper the next day when his mind was clear. Emily also suggested her brother reach out to Dr. Mary. Although Dr. Mary specialized in the research aspect of the writing process, Emily believed that she would be more than eager to help Brian to succeed.

The next day, Brian followed his sister's advice and called Dr. Mary. Once again, his "unofficial mentor" came to his rescue. Dr. Mary agreed to meet Brian at her office at the University of Scholars the following afternoon.

The following morning, as he did each day before leaving the house, Brian turned on the news to check out the current weather in his local area. To his surprise, severe thunderstorms were expected throughout most of the afternoon. Brian panicked; he vaguely remembered a conversation he had with Dr. Mary in which she had mentioned how much she despised driving in the rain. When the weather took a turn for the worst and the sky became darker and darker, Brian was sure that Dr. Mary would postpone their meeting until the next day. Even worse, Brian began having thoughts that he was not going to see Dr. Mary at all and that his paper would be submitted incomplete.

Fortunately, the strong downpour only lasted about ten minutes, so Brian and Dr. Mary were able to meet at the professor's office later in the day. When he arrived at her office, Brian let Dr. Mary read his mentor's comments.

"Hmm... Although I do not agree with her strong language and harsh approach, I can understand why your mentor felt the way that she did about your thesis. I don't want to scare you, but we will have to meet every day this week if you plan on handing in your thesis paper on time."

To start with, Dr. Mary told Brian to take out unnecessary facts and to add more information to support his argument that African-American women were a powerful force throughout the entire fight for women's suffrage. Appreciating and respecting her constructive criticism, Brian took Dr. Mary's advice and began to revise his thesis as soon as he arrived home that afternoon.

Over the next three days, the only times Brian stepped away from his computer were to eat, use the bathroom, and sleep. Brian pushed himself and put forth his best effort until he finally felt ready to submit his final thesis argument to be graded.

Every morning, Brian woke up and looked to see if his professor graded his paper. Exactly two weeks after submitting his thesis, Brian received an email notification that his thesis paper had been viewed and graded. This was the moment Brian had been waiting for. Before viewing his grade, Brian took a deep breath and said a quick prayer. He prayed to God that no matter the outcome, He knew that he worked hard on this paper. Upon opening the document, Brian saw that he received a "C-" on his paper and achieved a "B" in the class overall. Brian immediately began to cry tears of joy. Not only had he overcome his fear of writing, Brian could now leave all of his previous failures in the past and focus on his present self.

As Brian reflected on the many obstacles he had already faced and overcome, this by far would be one of the few that he would proudly remember for the rest of his life.

Now, Brian truly believed that he could make excellence happen throughout the rest of his life.

MEET THE AUTHOR

MERRIL E. HOLLOWAY II
AUTHOR. EDUCATOR. SPEAKER.
FOUNDER, MAKING EXCELLENCE HAPPEN

Merril E. Holloway, the younger of two children, was born to Bazola Holloway and Merril Holloway, Sr. As a "military kid" Merril travelled all over the world, including Turkey, England, France and Germany. His father served in the Army and gave his children the opportunity to experience and learn from different cultures. As a child Merril struggled with Reading and Writing, both elements that are necessary for successful communication in life. However, Merril never gave up on himself. After graduating from Frankfurt American High School in 1991, he began his college education at Prairie View A&M University studying Business. However, due to academic issues he transferred to Athens State University. At Athens State University, Merril began working towards his Education degree in 2000.

His studies took a unique turn in 2002 after a conversation with Merril's History Professor, Dr. Douglas Wertsch. As a result of their conversation and after much deliberation, Merril changed his major from Business to History and graduated with a History Degree in 2003. Merril believed that he was destined to reach people. So, in 2003 Merril went back to Athens State University to pursue his Education degree. He graduated with an Education Degree in 2006. After earning his teaching certificate, he became a classroom teacher. Merril craved more knowledge and went back to school to study for his Master's degree in American History.

Merril currently teaches at three colleges: Delaware Technical & Community College, Cecil College, and Wesley College. At Delaware Technical & Community College Merril is an Instructor in Political Science, Human Communication, First Year Seminar, and United States History I and II. At Cecil College he teaches Western Civilization I and II, American Government, and United States History I and II and at Wesley College he teaches United States History I and II.

Merril E. Holloway II believes that education and reading are essential tools critical to the success of all students. As a result, in 2011 he founded MEH: *Making Excellence Happen, a company that encompasses his passion for education.* His goal is to create an environment where children can reach for the stars and truly believe in themselves.

MEET THE PUBLISHER

http://www.whatawordpublishing.com

What A Word Publishing and Media Group is pleased to do our part to promote literary works globally.

We believe that everyone has a story to tell; each story as varied as our life experiences. We believe that each story can have a positive benefit and, in some cases, a life changing effect on another person's life. We also recognize the barriers to book writing and publishing that may confront an individual. To this end we offer Customized Book Coaching Services based on your Individual or Group needs, Book Publishing Seminars, Hands-On Workshops and other Author Book Events and resources. Our goal is to bring the book writing and publishing dreams of many to realization and to help you share your passion with others. To register for our Book Coaching, Editing and Publishing Services, Seminars and/or Workshops or to request information please contact Dr. Sheila Hayford, What A Word Publishing and Media Group via email at info@whatawordpublishing.com You may also visit: www.whatawordpublishing.com and fill out the "Contact Us" page.

To All of you,
Thank You!

Milton Keynes UK
Ingram Content Group UK Ltd.
UKHW050209250324
439991UK00013B/1621